500004069485

CU00325025

METROPOLITAN BOROU(

Please return this book to the Library fro.
before the last date stamped. If not in demand books may be renewed
by letter, telephone or in person. Fines will be charged on overdue
books at the rate currently determined by the Borough Council.

-- APR 2003

-- MAY 2004

GATES, S.

Beetle and the biosphere

592782

BEETLE AND THE BIOSPHERE

Books by the same author

Beware the Killer Coat!

For older readers

African Dreams
The Burnhope Wheel
Deadline for Danny's Beach
Dragline
The Lock

BEETLE
AND THE
BIOSPHERE

SUSAN GATES

Illustrations by
THELMA LAMBERT

WALKER BOOKS
LONDON

For Phil

First published 1994 by Walker Books Ltd
87 Vauxhall Walk, London SE11 5HJ

2 4 6 8 10 9 7 5 3 1

Text © 1994 Susan Gates
Illustrations © 1994 Thelma Lambert

The right of Susan Gates to be identified as author
of this work has been asserted by her in accordance with the
Copyright, Designs and Patents Act 1988.

This book has been typeset in Plantin.

Printed in England

British Library Cataloguing in Publication Data
A catalogue record for this book
is available from the British Library.

ISBN 0-7445-2466-0

Contents

Chapter 1

Abby grabbed her gun and fired it, *click*, *click*, *click*, into the plastic. She stepped back to check her work. It wasn't perfect. It wasn't at all like the thrilling plans that crowded her imagination. But it would do, for a start.

"Not bad," she told herself. "Not good. But not bad either."

The huge sheets of plastic rippled in the wind. Abby had fixed them together with the staples, then slung them, like a vast tent, between the sycamore trees in her grandma's back yard.

Abby thought her tent looked beautiful. The plastic gleamed like silver skin and the wind made it breathe as if it were alive.

But she was restless to move on. Already her thoughts, like giants in seven-league boots, were striding ahead, planning her next move and the move after that. Her experiment to save the world was only just beginning.

Abby didn't look the type to save the world. She looked too ordinary.

She was skinny, with a grave, unsmiling face – a colourless child with pale skin, pale eyes, pale lips, pale hair. But in her mind there were the wildest colours, the most extraordinary notions. And these ideas did not stay earthbound – they whizzed about among the stars and planets. They explored the universe.

The trouble came when she tried to tie them down, make them practical. Like she was doing now in Grandma Spooner's back yard.

But it was working out better than most of her schemes. So far, anyway.

"Got a lot to do yet," she murmured as she fired one last staple, for good measure, into the shimmering folds of plastic.

Abby put down her gun. She ripped open the entry flap, secured with Velcro, and stepped into the glittering structure she'd designed and built. She sealed the door carefully behind her.

From the outside, all that you could see

was the outline of her ghostly figure as she moved about here and there, busy with her own mysterious enterprise.

It was half an hour before she came out again and headed into the sand dunes, on a ladybird hunt. Ladybirds were an essential part of her plan to save the world.

There was one! A ladybird in smart red, black-spotted armour scuttling out from a sea holly.

"Got you!"

Abby cupped her hand over him, feeling him tickling her fingers. Then she blew the sand grains off him and popped him into her box.

Soon she had twenty-two of them. Abby watched her captives trundling about like tiny tanks. It was getting crowded in there.

"Time to get some breakfast," she told herself, closing the matchbox.

She straightened up, shading her eyes. The breeze, coming over the dunes from the sea, had a salty tang.

"It's going to be a beautiful day," thought Abby.

From here she could see Grandma Spooner's house with the tin roof glinting. It was one of half a dozen summer houses tucked into the dunes. They were hardly more than wooden shacks and had been known as the "Ramshackles" as long as anyone could remember. Even local maps had the Ramshackles marked on them.

"I'll have peanut butter sandwiches," decided Abby, as she started back to Grandma's house.

No one could call the dunes beautiful. Here and there was a hollow of fine white sand sprinkled with pink and yellow snail shells. But mostly the hills were scrubby with sea buckthorn and hawthorn. Razor-sharp grasses sliced your ankles. Rabbits left droppings everywhere in neat little piles that grew white and crumbly with age.

"Or maybe a sugar and banana sandwich."

Abby was walking through a green

corridor. There were masses of these narrow tracks, crisscrossing the dunes, tunnelling through the spikiest vegetation. Abby knew them like the back of her hand. She spent most school holidays down here with Grandma Spooner.

"And a Coke."

A hand was resting in the middle of the mossy path.

Its fingers were white, curled up like a huge dead spider.

"Urgh!" Abby's whole body jerked in horror. She backed away from the clutching hand. And dropped her box of ladybirds.

There was an old man sprawled among the buckthorn bushes. The branches were splintered as if he had crash-landed there.

Queasy, with her stomach clenched up like a sea anemone, Abby tiptoed closer.

"It's a dead body," she whispered, appalled.

He looked dead. He looked as if he'd been here for ages. As if he were part of the dunes.

His white hair sparkled. It sparkled because busy spiders had already colonized it and the morning dew was glittering in their webs.

Cautiously, on wobbly legs, Abby plucked a thorny branch aside so she could see his face.

"Mr Robinson!"

It was her grandma's neighbour – the only person, apart from Grandma, who lived all year in the summer houses.

His eyes blinked open.

Abby's terror collapsed. Urgency took over.

"Mr Robinson! Mr Robinson!"

She knelt down on crunchy snail shells. She touched his face, to make him look at her. His skin was cold and clammy, like sand before the sun warms it. A big white moth, hidden in his hair, flopped into Abby's hand. He must have been lying here all night. Abby shook the moth into the grass.

"It's Abby, Mr Robinson. Abby from next door. What happened? What are you doing out here?"

His bleary eyes showed some recognition. He made a feeble movement with his hand. She'd never liked him much. Her grandma liked to talk. But this man hardly spoke. And he had a fierce, hawk-like face that used to scare her when she was little.

But he was so helpless now that she wasn't scared. Only anxious.

"I'll go and get some help."

"Wait! Wait!" His voice was croaky, as if he hadn't used it for a long time.

When he moved his head, he broke the cobwebs that tied his hair to the ground.

"Get my wallet! Out of my coat pocket!"

Abby hesitated.

"Go on!"

With clumsy, trembling fingers Abby pulled the wallet from his pocket. It was made of battered leather, repaired with green cotton thread.

"Now give that to your grandma," he ordered roughly. "It's important. Go on, quick."

Abby stuffed the wallet in the back pocket of her jeans: "I'll go and get help." She began scrambling up the side of the dune.

"The wallet," he called out. "Don't forget the wallet. There's an important message in it. For Mrs Spooner."

But Abby didn't hear him. Skylarks shot up, twittering in alarm. Rabbits raced in all directions as she went crashing through the dune scrub towards the Ramshackles.

Mr Robinson tried to raise himself upon one elbow. But he was too weak. His head sank back onto a pillow of yellow dune poppies. He didn't move again.

The spiders carried on spinning their webs.

Hidden in a clump of sea holly, there were faint scrabblings in the matchbox Abby had dropped. It was twenty-two ladybirds, desperate to get out.

Chapter 2

Beetle sat alone in his grandpa's Ramshackle, waiting for the vandals to pay him a visit. They had been here three times in the past week. They had wrecked Mrs Freely's Ramshackle, two dunes away. Wrenched the boards off the windows, climbed inside and wrecked it.

"Don't worry, Grandpa," said Beetle. "I won't let anything happen to this place."

He didn't feel a fool talking to empty air. It made him feel less scared, acting as if Grandpa Robinson were still here, not lying on the other side of town in a hospital bed.

Beetle's mouth felt dry. He had never noticed before how much noise these old wooden shacks made, creaking and groaning as if they were trying to talk to you. Every fresh sound made him twitch.

"Concentrate!" he told himself severely. "You're supposed to be on guard, remember? Looking after things."

He squinted into Grandpa's telescope. Through its magnifying eye he could see far around, over the dips and swells of the grassy dunes and down to the sea. If he swivelled the telescope, he could see the other houses. Six in all, a little community of wooden shacks tucked into the wilderness of the dunes. Everyone in town knew this place as the Ramshackles. And he was known, by all his mates, as Beetle – although the reasons for this nickname were lost in the mists of time.

Beetle dropped the telescope.

"There's no sign of them yet, Grandpa."

He felt restless, shivery with apprehension. As far as he knew, all but one of the other Ramshackles were empty. Only his grandpa lived here all year round. Only his grandpa – and Mrs Spooner next door. Everyone else spent the summer here. But it was only May and the other shacks were still boarded up and padlocked. No one had arrived yet to open up the musty rooms to the warm winds from the sea.

"I'm bored now, Grandpa. I almost wish these vandals would come."

Creak. Beetle's head shot round. He shouldn't have wished that!

"Don't be stupid!" he mocked himself. "It's only the house, making noises."

He peered anxiously out of a window all the same.

"You are a prat," he told himself. "They probably won't come at all today."

Yesterday his grandpa had heard them as they smashed the window in Mrs Freely's Ramshackle. He had tried to catch them but had caught his foot in a rabbit hole and gone crashing down, hurting his leg. He had not even seen them, only heard branches cracking in the scrub as they escaped. And he had lain in the dunes all night, helpless, until this morning when somebody found him.

Beetle's thoughts were full of anguish. "I should have been with him. I promised him I'd be here yesterday."

But Beetle hadn't shown up. He'd gone round to his mate's house to watch a video rather than keep his grandpa company.

He was to blame for his grandpa's accident. If it hadn't been warm last night and his grandpa had died, frozen to death in the dunes, then he, Beetle, would have been to blame for that as well. He made his hands into fists and screwed them into his forehead, to drive out these monstrous thoughts.

To give himself courage, and something else to think about, he took his models out of his pockets. He had only brought a small selection. The rest were at home, with the fire dice and damage dice and event cards and all the other paraphernalia you needed to play Fantasy Adventure Games.

Beetle was a fanatical Adventure Gamer. Everywhere he went, he took a few of his favourite models with him. Today he had some elite warriors from the 39th Millennium. This one was Epidemon, a fearsome terminator robot, carrying a deadly plague-gas gun with a range of 20 cm. Epidemon was one of his best fighters, worth 200 points in the game, with 8 life points and a combat speed of 10 when he was mounted on his special rocket-powered Plague Buggy. Beetle hadn't managed to buy one of those – but he expected to in the near future. He was working on his mother for the money and although she hadn't broken yet, it was only a matter of time.

"Just play a quick game," Beetle told himself.

In the sunlight, on the bare boards of the Ramshackle floor, he began to set out his battle squadrons.

Anyone else looking at Beetle's 39th Millennium troops would have seen a jumble of metal and plastic miniatures – tiny painted toy figures. But Beetle didn't see them like that. When he was really involved in a game he saw vast futuristic armed forces – Imperial war machines versus Renegade robots, plus hordes of mutant creatures with tusks, claws and armoured wings, who slithered and flew after the main armies. His warriors had terrible weapons: plasma guns that turned the opposition into pools of slime, scorcher rays that sizzled them to a heap of smoking cinders.

"OK," Beetle instructed his men. "This is your mission. Intercept and eliminate! Knock out that Renegade base! Take no prisoners!"

You never took prisoners when you were an Adventure Gamer. You never had cease-fires, peace talks or any other negotiations.
It looked complicated. But basically it was simple. You had to blast the opposition before they blasted you.

"Move in Cryotron," said Beetle, shifting one of his little models a few centimetres across the floor.

Beetle knew the names of each warrior, of every weapon. This robot was called Cryotron. He had a deadly cryotronic triple blaster with targeter and a 100 degree field of fire. Its liquid-gas spray froze you instantly. You cracked into a pile of tiny cubes and tinkled to the ground, like a shattered windscreen.

This one was Secateur, a scuttling crab-like mutant Renegade whose only weapon was his huge ripper claws. He wasn't a very valuable warrior – only in close combat, and even then he could only scuttle sideways. He was worth a feeble 25 points and his leadership and initiative scores were 0.

"Doesn't matter if he gets zapped," decided Beetle, discussing gaming tactics with himself.

Lost in the 39th Millennium, in a future of blood-crazed clashing armies and horrific war machines, Beetle didn't hear the door of the Ramshackle creak open.

It creaked again. And this time, when he did hear it, even Cryotron wasn't powerful enough to give him courage. Beetle just crouched there, frozen in the middle of his armies, as if he'd been zapped by a cryotronic triple blaster.

"Who's there?" But his challenge was a whisper, fluttery as dry leaves blowing.

The Ramshackle sighed, the floorboards twanged. But he couldn't tell whether he hearing footsteps or not.

"Is anybody there?"

Sun flecks chased around him, swarming up the walls, over his armies and across the ship's bell, making it glitter like gold.

The ship's bell! When his grandpa retired, left the sea, he had saved that bell as a souvenir of his seafaring days. It was from an old coaster, the *Little Tern*. Beetle stretched out his hand towards the rope on the *Little Tern*'s bell and tugged it, again and again, filling the house and the lonely dunes beyond with the noise of its urgent clanging.

The back door slammed. The air quivered with the last echoes of the bell and then the echoes died...

Beetle shook his head to make his ears stop ringing. Then he got up, scattering his men. He even scrunched a warrior underfoot as he crept fearfully towards the tiny kitchen and the back door.

Nobody there. But the door was swinging open.

"You prat," he told himself. "It was only the wind." Trouble was, it was a dead calm afternoon.

But whoever it was (if it had been anybody at all) had been scared off by the clamour of the *Little Tern*'s bell.

"That was a good idea, that," he congratulated himself with a sickly, wobbling smile.

Braver now, Beetle peered outside. He didn't see the muddy boot imprint, freshly planted on the doorstep.

"There, I told you! There's nobody here, is there?"

Half a mile away, over the dunes, he could hear the faint slushing of the sea. But he couldn't see it because the grassy dunes rose high around him, folding the Ramshackles in their secret hollows. Nothing moved – except that next door, from Mrs Spooner's back yard, from her clump of four scrawny sycamores, he thought he caught a weird silver glow, like an alien spacecraft landing.

"Will you stop imagining things!" he fumed, rubbing his eyes. A cloud shunted over the sun. He looked again. There was nothing there now.

He closed the back door and bolted it. He made sure every window was shut tight. Then he took out his Predator robot – a supreme fighting machine, almost invincible. Just standing it on the palm of his hand gave him a surge of confidence. Eagerly he went back to his Adventure Game.

But he couldn't concentrate. The stuffy room made him sleepy. At one point, just as Predator was moving in to knock out the Renegade defence shield, Beetle suddenly dozed off, sprawling into the middle of his plastic models. And he dreamed a terrible dream.

He dreamed that Grandpa was dead –

Beetle's head jerked back. He woke up, staring about him, his eyes wide with horror, thinking that what he'd dreamed was true.

Then he looked down and saw that his

clenched right hand still gripped Predator –
worth 350 points in the game.

"Don't be such a wimp!" he mocked
himself. "Grandpa won't die, will he? Stands
to reason! He's only got a fractured leg.
He'll be out in a couple of weeks. Driving you
crazy again. Just like he used to."

But the dream lingered on, stubborn as a
bad smell. He pushed open a window to
flush it away. The dunes were striped with
long shadows. It was late afternoon. He
would have to go home soon, or his mum
would be worried.

"Have a last look round," he told himself as
he climbed up the ladder to his grandpa's tiny
attic bedroom.

This was Beetle's lookout post, where he
often came with his telescope. From here he
could see all the Ramshackles scattered
among the dunes.

Beetle really liked this place. Here he could
set out Predator and Cryotron and have
running battles that lasted days and days.

There was no fear of his mother tidying
them away or sucking them up in the Hoover.
Or he could just lie in the dunes in the warm
sandy slacks and watch the clouds race by.
Beetle liked to be relaxed, and the
Ramshackles, before the vandals came, was
the most relaxing place he knew.

"What's that!"

Beetle took the telescope away from his eye
so he could see better. At first, next door's
shack seemed no odder than usual. An old
woman lived there, harmless and dreamy,
Mrs Spooner, a retired biologist. Her garden
did not have flowers in it but driftwood and
interesting shells and bones – the skeletons of
things she'd picked up from the beach. Beetle
always found it creepy that such a mild, grey-
haired old lady could soak dead things in acid
until the flesh dissolved. He checked out
the grinning seal skull, the dolphin's ribcage,
the antlers of the drowned deer. Nothing
suspicious there.

But then, that silver flicker in the back yard

caught his eye and he remembered what he'd seen from the back door.

"Check it out!" he told himself excitedly and clattered down the ladder and out into the dunes.

Mrs Spooner had added to the skeletons in her front garden. A gleaming shark's jawbone yawned open, like a mantrap.

Where did she find that? he wondered briefly, as he edged past, keeping an eye on those wicked teeth.

Beetle rounded the back of Mrs Spooner's shack. What he found there drove jawbones from his mind. It had sprouted almost overnight, like a mushroom, on his territory, without him knowing anything about it. Beetle didn't like that.

"What a cheek!"

Beetle liked to be in control, to know what was going on. This giant silvery tent, closed and mysterious, made him immediately uneasy. Beetle didn't like strange or even unfamiliar situations. He liked routines and rules. He knew every fiddly rule of 39th Millennium warfare by heart. He was an expert.

Instinctively he groped around in his jacket pocket for Predator. But it seemed that, in his hurry, he'd forgotten to bring any of his models along. That upset him even more. It was bad luck to be without them. Even a lowly Scorpion infantry man with his deadly stinging tail (useless long-range but worth 6 in close combat) would have been some comfort now.

Beetle prowled suspiciously round the walls, poking at them so that the plastic rippled. He shoved his face up against them but he couldn't see through – it was all steamy inside. The walls were stapled along the joins and, at the top, nailed with wooden batons to the tree trunks. A plastic roof stretched over them. Not a thorough job.

Beetle tutted in disapproval. He enjoyed being thorough – he didn't like it when things weren't right. He painted his models himself, with finicking care. He was especially proud of Predator – glossy black with red and silver highlights. It had taken him hours to do. But this was a roughly made and fragile structure that shivered when you prodded it. One tug, and it would all come shimmering down – great waterfalls of plastic sheeting. Tempted, Beetle stretched out his hand.

And leapt back in shock. With a harsh ripping sound a split appeared in the tent side as someone's head bulged through.

"Aliens!" screamed Beetle's brain.

His alarm wasn't much diminished when he saw it was a girl – a skinny girl with a white, freckled face and a silver brace glinting on her top teeth.

"Who are you?" he challenged aggressively as if she had no right to be here on his home ground – his sand dunes, his Ramshackles.

She stepped outside and studied him with a severe and irritated gaze like teachers do when you interrupt their marking. That made Beetle even more uncomfortable. He wished that he'd got Cryotron to blast her to a heap of frozen chunks.

Finally she spoke. "If it's any of your business," she informed him coldly, "I'm a Biospherian. Who are you?"

Chapter 3

"What's this tent then?" demanded Beetle, gulping back a yawn.

Slyly he rattled the models inside his jacket pocket. To his relief, he'd just discovered two of them buried deep down under scrunched-up chocolate bar wrappers.

The girl was not a great talker. Beetle liked to talk – he was always opening his mouth and putting his foot in it. And it annoyed him that she hardly looked at him when she answered, as if she had more important things to think about.

"Can I see inside your tent?" he demanded, more out of a desire to make her pay attention to him than any interest in her silly games.

"It's a Biosphere, not a tent," Abby corrected him.

"Well, can I see inside your *Biosphere*, then?" asked Beetle irritably. He was not in a good mood. That dream about his grandpa being dead still prowled at the edges of his mind – he couldn't seem to chase it away. Just thinking about it made him shiver.

For the first time, the girl looked directly at him.

Then Beetle remembered that he'd seen her before, hanging round the dunes with Mrs Spooner. He flinched. Her eyes were unnerving; an unblinking pale grey stare that seemed to winkle out your deepest secrets, your nastiest habits. Beetle, who had several nasty habits, flushed uncomfortably. Now that she was looking at him, he wished she wasn't.

But he followed her into the Biosphere.

The heat whacked him in the face as soon as he entered.

The tent was high and spacious, as roomy as their lounge at home. "Wow!" gasped Beetle, staring up and so surprised that he forgot his uneasiness. "You've got trees in here!"

The lower branches of the sycamore trees were inside the tent, under the plastic roof. They were green and leafy, as if it was already summer.

It felt like walking into a steamy indoor forest. Sweat was trickling down Beetle's neck.

"Cool!" he exclaimed, to hide his bewilderment.

"They're for oxygen. The trees make oxygen. Or else we'd die in here."

"Oh, right," Beetle responded, nodding warily. And privately he thought: "Why can't I ever meet normal people?" All the girls he'd met seemed to fit into this category – not normal. He hadn't come across a single one who could appreciate Adventure Gaming. And this one even seemed a little crazy. He was glad he had Cryotron clenched in his left hand. You never knew with crazy people. Sometimes they were harmless, sometimes not.

Abby was darting here and there, showing him things. It was as if stepping inside the Biosphere had given her a surge of vitality. Even her pale cheeks were flushed. A splash of crimson drifted past Beetle's nose. It was a

Red Admiral butterfly, prisoner in the Biosphere.

"See," Abby was telling him, "they built a Biosphere in the desert in Arizona. I read all about it in Grandma's *New Scientist*. It's like this huge, airtight bubble made of glass and steel with an ocean and desert and forest inside it and lots of insects, plants and animals. And the Biospherians can live in there for years, breathing the oxygen made by the trees and plants, growing their own food and they never have to come out."

Beetle looked sceptically around the plastic tent. "This isn't a huge airtight bubble made of glass and steel," he pointed out. He didn't even bother wiping the smirk off his face.

But Abby didn't seem to hear the mockery in his voice. She shrugged regretfully. "Well, theirs is a multi-million dollar project. But I've only got my pocket money. So mine's just a simplified version – a kind of back yard Biosphere."

"That explains why it's so crap then," said

Beetle, stuffing his fist into his mouth to stop himself giggling.

But she was sharper than he thought. "You're a bit of a moron, aren't you?" she said suddenly to Beetle, turning her back on him as if he wasn't worth wasting time on.

"No, I'm not," protested Beetle, deeply offended. "No, I'm not a moron. I'm interested. Honest." He searched in his mind for a question to show his intelligence. The effort brought a scowl to his face. "So what are you growing to eat in here?" he asked finally. Despite his mirth, he'd already noticed that she'd cleared some spaces in the sandy soil. And that on the slightly sloping ground there was a freshwater channel collecting into a tiny pool and trickling out again under the tent wall.

"I've sown lettuces and cucumbers and tomato plants. That's for a start. It's not ready yet of course, not for me to live in. It'll take ages yet. I've only just started collecting the insects. I've got butterflies and bluebottles and spiders – I had some ladybirds as well but I lost them somewhere. It's hard work catching spiders. They run really fast—"

"Gross!" muttered Beetle, shuddering. He hated spiders.

"In the real Biosphere in Arizona they've got hummingbirds to pollinate the flowers – the Mexican rufous-tailed hummingbird, actually. But I'm going to catch some honey-bees instead."

She knelt down and dabbled her fingers in the clear water. "And I'm going to catch some fish for my pond. Get some more creatures and plants. When I've finished I'll have my own miniature planet inside this tent and everything in here that I need to survive. Just like the real Biospherians."

"Right," said Beetle, looking wise and nodding. He was still hurt that she'd insulted his intelligence. It reminded him of his teachers.

To get his own back, he tried to embarrass

her. "And where," he asked innocently, "do you go to the toilet when you're shut up in this Biosphere thing?"

Abby looked coolly at him. She had wondered when he would ask that question. "Well," she admitted. "I've been thinking about that. It's a fascinating problem."

"I mean," continued Beetle, with a wicked snicker, "after a few weeks you'd be knee-deep in—"

"Yes, I know," she interrupted him. "And I've been trying to work out a solution. I could pee into this stream here – "

She saw a startled look on Beetle's face. "No, no," she reassured him. "I mean *below* my freshwater supply and *below* my pond. And then, as it flows out, reeds that I could plant outside would absorb all the pollutants. Reeds do that, you know. I've read about it. But I've never tried it myself. It'd be dead interesting to try, don't you think?"

"Oh, dead interesting," said Beetle sulkily. He was deeply disappointed. She did not seem at all shocked – just intrigued by a scientific problem.

"And as for the other. Well, I'm working on that. I could recycle it – you can recycle human waste, you know – and use it for manure. It's a tough problem but I've been doing some experiments—"

"That's nice," interrupted Beetle, feeling queasy. He did not want to hear about the experiments she'd been doing.

"And I could even get some wild rabbits off the dunes. Use them for my food supply. They've got rabbits in the real Biosphere, in Arizona."

"Wait a minute," said Beetle, suddenly getting excited. "If you're going to live in here, never go outside – if you're going to eat these rabbits and fish, then you're going to have to kill them first, aren't you? You'll have to knock the fish's brains out, break the rabbits' necks with a karate chop." And he swiped at the air viciously to show her how to do it. "Look," he said. "It's easy. They don't feel a thing!"

It annoyed him that she didn't seem to be listening, especially now he was getting interested in this Biosphere business. She had taken a little box out of her pocket and opened it. A frenzy of bluebottles buzzed out and zoomed in all directions, batting themselves madly against the plastic walls.

"The most amazing thing," Abby was saying keenly, "is that a Biosphere, not this one, of course, but the real one in Arizona, could be used for space travel. You could live in space in a Biosphere, or set it up on another planet, like Mars, for instance."

"What! Do you mean that in the future, say the 39th Millennium or something, if the Earth was being destroyed by evil robots, for instance, that human survivors could escape in a Biosphere?"

"Well, yes," shrugged Abby.

"And they could set up an outpost on a distant planet?"

Abby nodded. "They might do."

"Wow," marvelled Beetle, as his mind boggled at the galactic implications of it all. He foresaw a whole new mission in his game – a whole new set of rules and tactics. Already he was assembling it in his head.

MISSION:

Planet Earth will no longer support human life. A small group of desperate men, women and children is trying to reach the Biosphere. Their plan, as the last surviving members of the human race, is to escape to Mars and found a colony. But their route is blocked by evil Renegade robots who seek to destroy them. Your mission, brave Imperial warrior, is to guide them through the Renegade blockade to the safety of the Biosphere. If you succeed, you will be a hero...

"I was telling you about the chickens they've got in the Biosphere in Arizona. Think I should get some chickens?"

"What?" he said to Abby grumpily, as if

she'd shaken him awake from a fascinating dream.

"Chickens. I was talking about chickens."

Beetle ignored that. He wasn't interested in chickens. He was pursuing his own line of thought.

"You know," he admitted to Abby, "I thought this was a rubbish idea at first. I mean, the way you first explained it."

But now he could appreciate its possibilities. "I'm interested in the future," he told her. He felt friendly and confidential towards her. He could see that they had more in common than he'd thought at first. "I'm really interested in things like this. I'm going to make a model of a Biosphere – I mean the real one in Arizona – and use it in my game."

"Game? What game?" asked Abby, baffled. To her, being a Biospherian wasn't a game. It was a serious scientific experiment.

"You mean you haven't heard of Adventure Gaming?" Beetle was already searching in his jacket pocket. He would show her Predator first and explain about his wicked claws that slice through body armour as easily as opening a can of spaghetti. She would be interested in that.

But he'd got no further than: "This is Predator, my favourite—" when he saw his grandpa's wallet sticking out of the back pocket of her jeans. "Where d'you get that?" Beetle bawled at her immediately, his face screwed up in outrage. "That's my grandpa's wallet, that is!"

She twisted round to see what he was looking at. "Oh, no! I was supposed to give that to my grandma. There's a message in it for her. But I forgot all about it… Was that your grandpa then, that I found in the dunes this morning?"

"You found him?" This was the perfect opportunity for Beetle to show his gratitude, to thank Abby for saving his grandpa's life. But Beetle didn't see things like that. All he could think of was that *she* had saved his grandpa's life instead of him.

He scowled at her jealously. "If Grandpa sent a message, he would have sent it to *me*!"

"He said my grandma. He said Mrs Spooner. I mean, he wasn't speaking very clearly. He was very groggy. But I'm sure he said to give it to my grandma."

"You didn't listen properly!" snarled Beetle. He glared at her defiantly, daring her to contradict him.

Abby shrugged. She was far too busy saving the world to bother about an old wallet. "Have it then."

Beetle snatched it from her.

In his frantic search through the compartments, some kind of purple papery stuff, thin as onion skins, fell out. Beetle ignored it. "There's nothing here," he wailed. "Wait a minute, wait a minute. I've found something!" It was a crumpled piece of paper.

Feverishly he smoothed it out. It wasn't in his grandpa's scrawly writing, as Beetle had expected. It had been torn out of a newspaper. There was an article, with a photograph beside it. A man's face filled the photo. It was a fleshy face with a wide, thin-lipped grin like a toad's.

Beetle had to flick the purple flakes away so he could read the words. When he reached the end, his howl of protest echoed through the Ramshackles.

"Look, look!" He thrust the piece of paper at Abby. "I can't believe it. Look what it says!"

Abby was planting lettuces. She wiped the soil off her hands, took the paper, sighed, and began to read.

CURE FOR COUNCIL'S HEADACHE?

VANDALISM AT THE RAMSHACKLES is becoming a major headache for the Council. "In the past few weeks," says Councillor Olive Green, "this remote spot has become a target for vandals. One of the shacks is now derelict. The place is in danger of becoming an eyesore. We will never win the Tidy Town competition next year if something is not done about the Ramshackles!"

One solution, which the Council is considering, is to sell the land. A buyer has already come forward: Mr Maurice Fishwick, who owns several amusement arcades in the town.

"I have big plans for the Ramshackles," says Mr Fishwick. "I intend to develop this run-down and neglected area. Make it somewhere the town can be proud of. I'll get rid of those old shacks for a start. When I've finished, no one will recognize the place. There'll be leisure facilities from one end of the dunes to the other!"

"Of course," added the enterprising Mr Fishwick, "I'm going to change the name. A name like the Ramshackles is hardly good for business, is it?"

Beside Abby, Beetle was hopping from one foot to the other in an agony of impatience.

"Did you read what he said? About getting rid of those old shacks? About changing the name? Who does he think he is? I hate that man!" cried Beetle, who had never heard of Maurice Fishwick before. "That's him in the photo, look! I hate his guts! I'm not going to let him bulldoze the Ramshackles. I'm going to stop him. That's why Grandpa sent *me* this message. He's depending on *me* to stop him!"

And he jabbed himself importantly in the chest to emphasize this point.

Beetle's eyes were gleaming. He had a clear mission to accomplish, just as in his Adventure Games. He ran it through his mind.

MISSION:

Engage and neutralize the evil Maurice Fishwick. If you succeed you will be a hero. You will become Supreme Commander. You will be honoured with the Imperium's highest award for bravery!

He turned to Abby. "OK, then," he said. "So what are me and you going to do to save the Ramshackles?"

Chapter 4

"He's not safe on his own in that house.
I mean, it's so out of the way, isn't it?"

"It was just sheer luck that someone came
along in time. We could be going to his funeral
today instead of visiting him in hospital."

"You can't trust him. You really can't. You
just don't know what he's going to do next!"

Beetle listened miserably to his mother and
his aunt talking about Grandpa, as if he were a
naughty child. They had already spoken about
"putting him in a home". Beetle said nothing.
But he deeply resented them discussing
Grandpa as if his mind were cracked, along
with his leg.

Grandpa had told him such stories about his
life at sea – about the reindeer in the
Norwegian fjords swimming across in front of
the ships, about dolphins doing somersaults in
the air as if they were on trampolines, about
the time they fished up a dead man in the nets
and played cards for his boots. Beetle shivered.
He didn't like thinking about dead men.

"How long have we been waiting here?"

complained his mother to his aunt. "Surely it's time for them to let us into the wards."

"There's five minutes to go yet." They were talking in whispers, as if they were in church. It made their voices sound creepy and unnatural and added to Beetle's apprehension. He was terrified, when those big doors finally swung open, of what he would see behind them—

"Beetle, pull your feet in!" his mother hissed at him. "People keep tripping over you."

Wretchedly, Beetle drew his knees up. He was huddled against the corridor wall with his 39th Millennium troops spread out on the green linoleum.

He'd left Abby back at the Biosphere. She'd promised to think about ways of saving the Ramshackles. Beetle didn't like her much but even *he* could see that she was good at ideas. She seemed able to pluck them out of thin air, like a conjuror whipping bunches of flowers from up his sleeve.

To comfort himself, Beetle began moving his model warriors about. And soon the voices, yakking on above his head, grew fainter and fainter as he plunged deeper and deeper into the 39th Millennium...

Sonicator, latest addition to the Imperial forces, was on the move. His mission: to lead the ragged band of survivors, the only humans left on Earth, through the Renegade troops to the safety of the Biosphere. Sonicator turned to face the enemy. The satellite dish on his chest tilted slowly. He was focusing on his target. With a low menacing hum, beam after beam of high-energy vibrations smashed into Epidemon, who blocked their way to the Biosphere. The humans could see it just beyond him – a vast space transporter, big as a small town, that carried, under its glass dome, the last trees and plants and animals from a planet where trees no longer grew. Epidemon began to shake. The menacing hum increased to a ferocious whine. He struggled to aim his plague-gas weapon. But bits of his body armour began to clatter to the ground and roll away, like car hubcaps. He was disintegrating into a great heap of scrap metal.

"Watch out!" muttered Beetle.

From behind the Biosphere, waving his metal claw to challenge the intruders, Secateur scuttled out sideways.

Sonicator, guardian of the last humans on Earth, levelled his deadly sonic weapon—

"Beetle, will you get out of the way? People are trying to get past."

Beetle stared up, blinking, dazed, as if he'd been accidentally beamed through a time warp into this gloomy hospital corridor. Slowly he collected up his troops and pocketed them.

As the doors opened, a whiff of hospital disinfectant scoured the last remaining traces of the 39th Millennium from his brain.

Reluctantly he trailed along behind his aunt and mother into the ward. He stared about him nervously while they spoke with a nurse in a blue uniform. Although he had Predator clutched in his hand, his dread was as sharp now as it had been after his awful nightmare. He felt hot and sick. The collar of his shirt felt tight...

But his mother and aunt were clattering up the ward, purposeful, business-like, as if they knew where they were going. He hurried after them, keeping his head down.

They stopped. He almost collided with them.

"Shh!" shrilled his aunt in a whisper loud enough to wake the dead. "He's fast asleep. Like a baby. Bless 'im!"

Fearfully, Beetle tilted his head to study his grandpa's face. They had shaved him so that his skin was smooth and white, not grey and stubbly. It was strange to see his features so calm and still as if he were made out of wax. Usually his grandpa's face was creased up with expressions – curious, amused, stubborn or angry.

But it was him all right. And he was breathing, snoring even. He certainly wasn't dead. Beetle felt dizzy with relief.

His grandpa's plastered leg was hidden away under the bedclothes. Beetle lifted up a corner of the sheet to look at it. And he had the sudden, wild idea of writing a message on it so his grandad would see it when he woke up and know that Beetle had been visiting.

"Put that sheet down!" snapped his mother, her eyes darting anxiously along the ward. "A nurse might see you!"

Beetle scowled. "I was only looking!"

"Well, don't look. Behave yourself. You're in a hospital, remember!"

"Grandpa is all right though, isn't he?"

"Course he is!" said Beetle's aunt. "Take more than a broken leg to kill a cantankerous old goat like him!"

Beetle allowed a tiny grin to flicker across his glum face. But he still wasn't sure whether or not to believe her.

"Might as well go then," said his mother. "Seems a pity to disturb him." She sounded relieved. Secretly, Beetle felt relieved as well. Now that he'd convinced himself that his grandpa wasn't dead, all he wanted to do was escape from this stuffy ward, into the sunshine.

But he lingered behind, until his mother and aunt were out of sight. He could hear their loud voices greeting someone they'd just recognized.

Looking shiftily around him, Beetle drew a red felt-tip pen from his trouser pocket and lifted the sheet at the end of the bed. There were many things he wanted to write on his grandpa's leg. He wanted to write: *Sorry I wasn't there the night the vandals came*. And he wanted to write: *Don't worry, I won't let them take your house away*.

There wasn't time. So he just scrawled:

See Locker!

But he placed his hand on the plaster cast and made a solemn promise. "I, Beetle, will save the Ramshackles!" he whispered.

He dropped the sheet and, scrabbling in his pocket, took out Predator, his very favourite 39th Millennium warrior, and placed him gently on the locker beside the glass of water. It was in Beetle's mind that if Predator gave him strength, then it would work for his grandpa too. His grandpa would appreciate the value of that gift and know how hard it was for Beetle to leave Predator behind.

Without looking back, Beetle raced down the ward, wincing as his trainers squeaked on the linoleum. Then he hurried through the swing doors and was gone.

Chapter 5

Gloomily Beetle swatted at a Red Admiral
butterfly. It had landed on his coat, thinking
he was a flower. It drifted away again.

He was back in the Biosphere, sweating in its
jungly heat with the silvery walls quivering
round him.

"So I told Grandma," Abby was saying,
"and she said that it's obvious what
Maurice Fishwick will do. You see, all the
Ramshacklers own the houses, but they
pay rent on the land. So he'll just buy the
land from the Council, then push up rents so
high that nobody will be able to afford
them. So everyone will sell their Ramshackles
to him – for peanuts. And then he'll flatten
the whole lot."

"What did you tell her for?" grumbled
Beetle jealously. "I saw her just now, cleaning
those shark's teeth with a toothbrush. She's
batty, she is!"

"She's a marine biologist," said Abby, as if
that explained everything. "And she says that
we'll have to write letters to the newspapers,

get organized. She's phoning up the other Ramshacklers, arranging a meeting. She's already started making a banner with SAVE OUR RAMSHACKLES on it."

"Well, that's useless, that is!" bellowed Beetle. "Who's going to see it right out here? Only seagulls and rabbits!"

Behind his rage lay the dreadful fear that Mrs Spooner might save the Ramshackles before he did. He wanted to do it so that his grandpa would be proud of him. He wanted to prove that he was reliable and could be trusted.

"What good is making a stupid banner going to be? We need some action. We need to kick some ass!" Beetle liked this expression. He'd heard it on an American TV programme. Just using it made him feel tough.

Abby wasn't really listening. She was worried about the Biosphere. Things were going badly wrong. It was too hot inside, for a start.

Things were dying. Yesterday she'd found some of her rarest butterflies dead – shrivelled blue corpses, light and flimsy as airmail paper. There were clusters of greenfly everywhere, even in the trees above their heads. They were killing all the plants. She should never have lost those ladybirds – they would have munched up those greenfly in no time at all. But the greenfly had taken over, multiplying like mad in the heat, dripping sticky honeydew over everything. Now black mould was growing on the honeydew. Things were getting out of control. The Biosphere was beginning to stink.

Even the tadpoles in the pond were dead. She'd found their bodies this morning, black blobs of jelly tangled up in green slime.

An idea whizzed across her mind like a shooting star.

"Do you think," she said eagerly to Beetle, "that if I could find some kind of fan, say a car radiator fan or something – no, no, if I could find two of them – that I could have one outside, turning in the wind, and it would drive one inside with a kind of pulley and circulate the air in here. Make it cooler?"

"You're supposed to be thinking about saving the Ramshackles!" complained Beetle. He was hot and tired and in a bad mood. "I mean, I couldn't think about it, could I? I was busy. I had to go to the hospital, didn't I?"

But Abby was already sketching plans for her cooling system in the soil with a stick.

"I promised my grandpa!" Beetle roared at her. "I made a promise on his leg!" Automatically he reached inside his jacket pocket for Predator, then realized he'd left him in the hospital. This made him even more depressed.

"I'm going outside!" he muttered, flouncing out of the Biosphere.

At first he thought that Abby wouldn't follow. But she did. In fact she was relieved to be out of the Biosphere. The responsibility of keeping things alive in there was weighing heavily on her. She had imagined it lush and green, like the photographs she'd seen of the Biosphere in Arizona. There was no mould there, no slime, no sticky, stinking dead things.

"What's this doing here?" said Beetle sulkily, kicking a dustbin lid out of his way.

"Oh, that." Abby looked at it vaguely. "It's my last experiment. I was going to make it into a Solar Furnace. But then I got interested in Biospheres."

Beetle picked up the dustbin lid. He held it in front of him like a shield and began fighting, parrying imaginary sword thrusts: "Die, you scurvy knave!"

Abby sighed. Her first impression of Beetle, that he was a complete airhead, was only strengthened by this childish display.

"Look," she said in long-suffering tones. "That's a serious experiment, that is, to use energy from the sun. A Solar Furnace concentrates the sun's rays into a point and where that point is, it's hot enough to boil water, to fry an egg."

"Oh, yeah," said Beetle, yawning rudely and

scuffling his feet in the sand.

But Abby was pleased to be thinking about something else other than the Biosphere.

"I'd have to cover the dustbin lid with tinfoil first," she said, "to make it really shiny. In Colorado they have these massive reflecting dishes big as houses, but I've— "

"Only got my pocket money," finished Beetle, sniggering.

"See. This is how it works. I'll give you a demonstration."

Eagerly, Abby took a small, round mirror from her pocket. "This is a tiny Solar Furnace. It's a curved mirror – I borrowed it from Grandma's microscope."

She tilted the mirror at the grass and waited. It became a dazzling badge of light as the sun hit it.

"Nothing's happening!" jeered Beetle.

"Wait!" Abby's face was tense with concentration.

The grass, dry as old bones from lack of rain, began to shrivel and grow brown and crisp. A tiny curl of smoke rose from the scorched blades. Abby leapt up and stamped the grass into a black smudge: "Don't want to start a fire!"

"I know what it is!" cried Beetle. "It's a death ray, isn't it?" He thought of Sonicator and his satellite dish, his deadly sonic beam that vibrated enemy robots into bits. Only this was a heat beam, not a sound beam. He understood it now!

"What a brilliant weapon!" he cried, inspired.

"It's not meant to be a weapon," objected Abby.

But Beetle was leaping around. This was the kind of action that he craved. He couldn't wait to see the death ray work. "We wouldn't kill them," he gabbled, "just singe them a little bit. Scare them off."

"Who are you talking about?" asked Abby desperately.

"The vandals, of course. Who do you think!"

Chapter 6

"Is this really going to work?" asked Beetle the following morning.

"Theoretically," answered Abby. "But I've had to improvise a lot with the materials. I mean, the Solar Furnace in Colorado didn't use tinfoil and a dustbin lid. It was a multi-million-dollar project."

She didn't know why she'd let Beetle talk her into this. They were both flattened into a scoop of warm sand, spying down on the Ramshackles. They were waiting to scare off the vandals. Beetle's idea was: stop the vandals, so the Council would have no excuse to sell off the sand dunes and the Ramshackles would be saved. Beetle was pinning all his hopes on this. It was his only plan.

But already Beetle was getting bored. He was no good at waiting and being patient. Slyly he slipped Epidemon from his jacket pocket.

"Time for a quick intergalactic war," he told himself.

"I think it's ready now," said Abby.

Beetle brightened up. This experiment looked quite impressive – all glittering silver foil.

"OK," said Abby. "Here we go. But don't get impatient. It's going to take a while to get the focus right."

She picked up the silver dustbin lid and jiggled it around. As the sun struck it, it burst into glowing life, like a brilliant flower blooming.

Beetle's nose parted the razor grass.

A small boy was wandering along a dune track. He was eating an ice-cream. Directly beneath them the ice-cream melted, gloop, all down his arm.

Beetle yelled in triumph. "It's working. It's working!"

"I didn't do that!" said Abby scornfully. "I haven't even aimed it yet."

"Oh." Beetle was disappointed. Suddenly, compared to a cryotronic triple blaster, this seemed a puny weapon.

They waited. It was very hot. The sun

clanged off the sand as if the dunes were a great golden gong. Beetle's head ached.

A skylark catapulted out of the grass. Even when it was a speck in the sky they could still hear its warbling song. "I could have had skylarks in my Biosphere," thought Abby.

She hadn't meant to think about the Biosphere! She hadn't been inside it at all today. She was scared of going in there, of seeing those papery butterfly corpses so frail and withered that even your breath would lift them off the ground. She was scared of the stink of death and decay that would hit her as soon as she opened the door.

"More people coming," murmured Beetle.

Two boys. They were shambling along. One of them was lashing about him with a stick, lopping the heads off the sea pinks. Nothing suspicious about that. Beetle liked doing that himself. Even when one of them, the skinny blond one with limbs like a stick insect, kicked out at Grandpa's dustbin, Beetle was only mildly indignant. He always kicked that dustbin as he passed. It made a satisfying clang.

Suddenly the freckled one with a pale face and reddish hair bolted off, sliding down a dune towards Mrs Spooner's Ramshackle. Beetle felt a twist of unease in his stomach. Automatically he felt in his pocket for Predator, forgetting that he wasn't there...

Red-hair was running now, arms whirling like windmills to keep his balance. Stick Insect plunged after him.

"It's them," gasped Beetle. "It's the vandals!"

They began by kicking Mrs Spooner's bones. Gleefully they crunched the fragile shell of a seal skull. They hurled a jawbone like a boomerang. Then they turned their attention to her other biological specimens. They cracked a beautiful pink-flecked conch shell into shards and ground delicate trees of coral into powder under their heels.

"Use it! Use the death ray!"

Now they were crushing sea urchin shells

in their great fists! Beetle couldn't stand it.
He was a sand dune child. He knew how hard
it was to find unbroken urchin cases, how
long you had to search. And these were
perfect, pure white, flimsy as blown eggs.
Beetle had held one once, cupped in the palm
of his hand.

"Blast them with the death ray!" he hissed
at Abby.

"It's not working," said Abby, flustered,
fiddling with the Solar Furnace. "It's the
wrong size, the wrong shape or something.
I'll have to take it back to the planning stage,
rebuild it."

"There's no time for that!"

Beetle rocked to and fro in anguish, his
insides scrunched into a tight little knot. They
were older, taller and stronger than he was.
Their frenzied attack on Mrs Spooner's bones
scared him stiff. But he had to do something
– he had promised on his grandpa's leg.

With a wild desperate cry, he leapt up from
his hiding place. "Stop doing that!"

But they didn't hear him. They were having too much fun.

They were prowling round the Biosphere now, poking at its walls, trying to peer inside. Red-hair ripped open the Velcro flap and swaggered in, Stick Insect on his heels.

Beetle began to scramble down the dunes towards them...

Black slime smeared Red-hair's hands. He tried to scrape it off but, tacky as chewed gum, it just spun out into long elastic strands.

"Ugh!"

Something squelched under Stick Insect's boot. "It stinks!"

It stank to high heaven – of hot, wet, rotting things.

Black gobs dribbled in their hair. Everything was covered with a sooty mould. It dripped from the branches of the trees in gluey tears, looped from grass stem to grass stem, smothered every surface in an inky crust.

"Let's get out of here!"

But the Velcro door had sealed itself up and all the sweating silvery walls looked just the same.

The plants, the insects – everything that Abby had so carefully collected was gummed up in a slimy shroud.

Red-hair looked up. A sticky thread unravelled from a tree branch and plopped into his mouth.

"Ugh! Ugh!" Choking, he tried to spit it out. Slipping on rotting leaves and horrid slithery things, the two boys fought to escape. Wildly Stick Insect hurled himself again and again at the walls.

"Get me out of here!"

Then, just as Beetle panted up to the Biosphere, Stick Insect and Red-hair came bursting out of it.

They scarpered, both of them. Beetle gaped after them. He shook his head in helpless, tongue-tied wonder.

Frantic skylarks exploded from the scrub,

rabbits hurtled everywhere. The last Beetle
saw of them was Stick Insect, gobbling
up the skyline with his spindly scissoring
legs. He plummeted down a dune and
was gone.

Beetle felt brave, heroic even, as if he'd
scared them off.

"Look at that!" he boasted as Abby came
skidding down the dune carrying the Solar
Furnace. "What a pair of wimps!"

Then he had a brilliant idea. It arched
across his mind like a rainbow, surprising him
with its splendour. "I'm going to follow
them! I'm going to find out where they live.
So we can tell the police!"

And he was off, before Abby could argue.
Sighing, she propped the Solar Furnace on
the grass beside the Biosphere and went to
view the wreckage of her grandma's
collection. Gran would be back from town
soon. Abby tried to piece the shattered conch
together, as if it were a broken teapot.

Behind her back, as the sun slid above the

sycamores, the Solar Furnace flared into life,
like a blazing beacon.

Beetle's breath came in great whooping gasps
as he staggered up the sides of dunes then,
with his arms out like a surfer, hurled himself
down slopes. Beetle wasn't a natural athlete.
He was the kind of boy who shivered in baggy
shorts on the edge of the football field.
But a glimpse of a bobbing red splash in the
distance drove him on. It was Red-hair.
They were heading towards town. He would
lose them if he didn't catch up.

Beetle ran as he had never run before,
smashing his way through bushes until he
found a track, scuttling along it, then left onto
another, diving through a tunnel under a
hawthorn bush, springing up, running again.

Once he tripped – somersaulted down a
slope. Landed in the deep dark pit of a slack
with cold sand beneath his cheek. For ten
seconds he lay there, stunned, breath battered
from his body. Then he was up and off again.

Behind him, where he'd fallen, lay a heap of tiny metal men: Cryotron, Sonicator, Epidemon. Throughout the night, as the wind blew, the shifting sand would bury them, grain by grain. By morning there'd be no sign of them at all.

Beetle crashed out of the dunes onto an open beach. Across the road were houses, shops and cafés. There were people about. Beetle hobbled on, doubled up from a scorching pain in his left side. His legs felt floppy, as if the bones inside them had dissolved.

But he could still see Stick Insect and Red-hair. He hadn't lost them. Beetle gave a sickly grin of triumph.

Then – where were they? Wildly Beetle stared about. They'd vanished from the street. He dodged between cars and ended up outside an open doorway like the black mouth to a cave. He plunged inside.

It was an amusement arcade – full of burbling electronic music, eerie blue and orange light, shadowy figures crouched over machines. Beetle melted into the noisy dark.

In a glass cage, in the middle of the arcade, sat Maurice Fishwick. Beetle recognized that fleshy face and wide toady smirk from the photo in the newspaper. He was giving people change for the machines. He seemed even fatter than in his photo, crammed into his glass cage, overflowing his chair. And his flesh was dead-white, as if he never went outside in daylight.

Red-hair and Stick Insect sidled up to the cage. They looked like wrecks, their clothes and hair sticky with black slime. Inside the glass a pudgy hand closed on money. It sent a cascade of golden coins clattering down a chute. Stick Insect and Red-hair raked them up, stuffed them in their pockets. Words were whispered through the grill.

Beetle's jaw hung slack in amazement. Inside his head a dazzling light clicked on. He understood it now!

"He's paying them!" he whispered to

-85-

himself. "Paying them for what they've done!"

Dazed by this knowledge, he hardly noticed Red-hair and Stick Insect slip away. He'd lost his chance to follow them. Other customers queued up at the cage, taking money, whispering through the grill, just as they had done.

Beetle shook his head in confusion.

"You might be wrong," he thought. But a moment ago he'd been absolutely sure that he was right.

Blinking, he emerged into the sunshine and began the weary trek back to the dunes.

He was fed up. His mission to save the Ramshackles and make his grandpa proud of him was falling apart. He'd let Red-hair and Stick Insect escape and now he wasn't even sure what he'd seen back there in the twilight world of the arcade. Even if Maurice Fishwick was hiring vandals to wreck the Ramshackles, Beetle didn't have any proof.

"Huh!" Beetle dragged a deep despondent sigh from the bottom of his boots.

He felt helpless. He didn't know what to do next. In Adventure Gaming everything was set out for you. The Rule Book told you what to do next. If you were confused, all you had to do was consult the rules. Beetle wished real life was more like Adventure Gaming. He wished he had a rule book to tell him how to save the Ramshackles and make his grandpa proud of him.

Instinctively he reached into his pocket for Epidemon. And discovered, to his horror, that his best warriors were gone! He searched in all his pockets. He turned them inside out.

"Oh, no!" Beetle's desolate wail made people turn to look at him.

It was the last straw. Sick despair engulfed him. He felt weak, as if all his strength had drained away.

He trudged on, sunk in gloom. Sometimes he pounced on a heap of sand and scrabbled away like a dog digging holes. But he couldn't find his men.

"It's useless!" He flopped onto a pad of

moss, itchy with sweat and exhausted.

"Wait a minute!"

He'd found something! Feverishly he hauled it up in a handful of sand. But as the grains trickled away through his fingers he saw it was only a matchbox with holes peppered in the lid. He shook the box. It rattled. Faint scratchy sounds came from inside.

He clambered to his feet and was just about to open it when –

"What's that!"

Something was darkening the sky over by his grandpa's Ramshackle. Beetle squinted into the sun. The tin roof had tendrils of smoke writhing all over it like some evil climbing plant.

"Fire!" bawled Beetle.

And, dropping the matchbox in the sand, he began to run.

Chapter 7

"Fire!" yelled Beetle again, although nobody could hear him but the skylarks. And he ran on, clumsily, floundering through the fine white sand.

"Please, please, please, please, please," were the words that sobbed through Beetle's brain in time to his gasping breaths. That meant: "Please don't let my grandpa's Ramshackle be a burnt-out ruin when I get there."

He abandoned the grassy tracks and crashed through blackthorn bushes. Banded snail-shells crunched to powder as he pounded down the slopes. As he got closer he could smell the smoke. A column of it hung in the blue sky. It was black and thick and oily and smelled of...

"Plastic!" said Beetle wonderingly to himself as he burst into the clearing.

It was not his grandpa's Ramshackle but the Biosphere that was alight. Shrinking away before his eyes, the walls were blistering and melting. There were huge gaping holes in them and on the charred grass were spreading pools of burning molten plastic. Tiny flames licked over them.

Beetle, in a frantic war dance, began stamping out the grass. But the flames had climbed the trees and were racing, like fiery squirrels, along the branches. Mrs Spooner, white hair in a frizz, was struggling to lift a bucket from the standpipe. Beetle dashed over, heaved it up and staggered to the fire. The plastic hissed, and steam rose up in clouds as he hurled the water. Coughing as the smoke snatched at his throat, Beetle ran back to the tap.

Only Abby stood by, looking on, tiny fires reflected in her eyes as she stared at the tatters of the Biosphere. Blobs of plastic pattered down like hailstones. But still she didn't move.

"It's going out," said Mrs Spooner, dragging her hand across her grimy face.

Beetle tossed water in a gleaming arc onto the blackened wreck. One last feeble spurt and the flames collapsed.

The sun, a pale disc, was dimly visible through the smoky haze. And then they could see blue. The sky had cleared. Beetle stopped coughing. Some people shouted from the top of a dune, and as they hurried down Mrs Spooner tramped wearily up to meet them.

"It's all right," he could hear her explaining. "Just a little fire. We managed to put it out by ourselves."

"Thank you, thank you, thank you," muttered Beetle, because his prayers had been answered and his grandpa's Ramshackle had not been harmed.

But then he felt guilty. He'd forgotten about Abby. He turned awkwardly to try and comfort her. Her Biosphere was a total write-off. All that remained was a rough circle of sooty stones, the stones that had weighted down the walls. Apart from a few gluey puddles it was the only evidence that the Biosphere had ever existed. Inside the circle, there was crunchy, blackened vegetation that crumbled into ashes even as they watched.

"Sorry," said Beetle. He could not tell, from Abby's blank face, what she was thinking. Perhaps, he thought, she was in a state of shock.

But she wasn't shocked. She wasn't even sorry. She just felt relief, as if a dreadful responsibility had drifted off into the summer sky along with the smoke. It was as if the whole stinking mess had been scorched clean by fire.

Beetle, though, concluded that she was desperately unhappy. He hopped about, embarrassed, from one foot to another. He wanted to say the right words but he couldn't think of what they were.

"It was the Solar Furnace," said Abby briefly, "that set the grass alight. And then the Biosphere melted."

"Oh," said Beetle, nodding sympathetically. And then he had an idea.

"Look," he said in a rush of words. "I'll help you. I'll help you build another Biosphere."

-94-

"Thanks," she said. "That's really kind of you. But I don't think so."

Beetle flushed, shuffling with embarrassment. No one had ever, in his entire life, called him kind before.

Mrs Spooner came back down the dune. She was pale and slight like Abby, dressed in denim dungarees, saggy as a walrus skin – she wore them all the time. She had always seemed to Beetle a bit vague, a bit dreamy, fussing about on the beach collecting things. But there'd been nothing vague about the way she'd tackled that fire. And when she came close he could see she had the same disconcerting eyes as Abby – eyes that didn't tolerate fools. Beetle, who'd been called a fool on more than one occasion, flinched from those eyes.

But when she spoke, her voice sounded worn-out. "We were lucky there," she said. "Lucky that the Ramshackles didn't catch fire. Though I suppose it would have saved Mr Fishwick the job of knocking them down."

"What do you mean?" demanded Beetle, his voice twanging with suspicion.

"Well, didn't you see the local paper last night? The deal to sell the dunes is going ahead. The Council is considering Mr Fishwick's offer."

"Oh, no!" wailed Beetle. "My grandpa's coming out of hospital on Saturday. What am I going to tell him? I made a promise on his leg!"

"We'll carry on fighting!" declared Mrs Spooner, lifting her sharp little chin defiantly. "We won't give up! I'm writing a letter to County Hall!"

But Beetle had already slouched off, to brood in Grandpa's Ramshackle. "Writing letters!" he muttered bitterly to himself as he slammed the door. "What use is that!"

He didn't even have the heart for Adventure Gaming. He'd lost all the warriors that mattered to him – the deadliest and most powerful. The ones who could reduce enemies to frozen chunks or molten puddles with one blast of their weapons.

He still had Secateur, the mutant crab. But a mobile can-opener (worth a feeble 25 points) that can only scuttle sideways was hardly much help in a crisis.

"Huh!" sighed Beetle, in deep disgust at the state of the world.

Exhausted, he slumped onto Grandpa's sofa – the one with the creaking springs that was draped in an old patchwork quilt. Beetle had always liked that quilt. It was deep blue, red and green – it glowed with colours like a stained glass window. He wrapped himself in it for comfort, fingering the silky edges as he did with a favourite blanket when he was a baby. If he had caught himself doing that he would have been horrified. But he was too tired to notice.

He fell asleep, clutching the quilt, while all around him the old shack murmured and groaned softly. Half a mile away over the dunes the sea shushed onto the beach. The tide was creeping in.

Chapter 8

"Is that Beetle up there?" whispered Mrs Spooner.

Abby was out in the back yard, tidying up the burnt-out Biosphere. She was clearing away all the cindery pieces of plastic. Only a patch of scorched earth showed where the Biosphere had been. Already, fresh green plants were springing up from the blackened soil.

Abby glanced slyly upwards. "Yes," she said. "He's terrible at hiding, isn't he?"

"Why doesn't he come down?"

Abby shrugged. "Because he's sulking."

But both of them knew that it was more than that. They had guessed that Beetle felt such black despair because he felt helpless to save the Ramshackles.

For ages Beetle had hardly talked to anyone. At home they said: "Just ignore him. He's in one of his moods." He'd passed the days at the Ramshackles, peering down from Grandpa's attic bedroom, or flitting along the dune tracks like a grouchy ghost.

The half-term holiday was almost over.
On Monday it was school again.

He refused to go and see his grandpa in hospital. "He's asking about you," his mother said. "He wants to know why you haven't been to see him." But Beetle knew that if he went he would have to confess that the deal to buy the dunes was going ahead. That he, Beetle, had made no more impression on events than a feather on a stone.

He'd dismally failed in his mission to save the Ramshackles. All his swaggering and boasting and wild promises on broken legs had come to nothing. Beetle felt angry and hopeless – and very sorry for himself.

One by one the Ramshacklers returned in cars piled up with luggage. Windows were unboarded and flung open to flush out the stale air. Beetle could smell onions frying, hear shouts and laughter. People crisscrossed the dunes to greet each other and talk tactics.

SAVE OUR RAMSHACKLES posters appeared in all the windows.

But still Beetle stayed out in the cold, being miserable.

Today was Saturday morning. Grandpa was due home this afternoon. Beetle should have tidied up the Ramshackle – cleared away all the mutant warriors, shaken out the quilt, polished the *Little Tern*'s bell, things like that – so that everything would be bright and welcoming for his grandpa's return. But instead he'd spent the morning just slouching around in the dunes.

Half-heartedly he scooped a hole in the sand, looking for his warriors. He'd given up all hope of finding them.

"What's this?" he wondered.

It was the matchbox.

"Not that again!"

But this time, Beetle opened it. It was crammed full of ladybirds.

He tipped them out on the sand. They stayed where they were, like tiny upturned turtles. At first he thought that they were all dead. Some of them were. But one flipped over and trundled off into the razor grass. Another, like a climber on Mount Everest, started to scale the dune.

"This is ridiculous!" declared Abby down in Mrs Spooner's back yard. "Him hiding up there, watching us!"

She moved out from under the sycamores into the sunshine. "Come down here, Beetle!" she yelled.

Beetle poked his nose through the razor grass. He looked down longingly. He ached for some company. The last week had been the loneliest of his life.

"Come on!"

And suddenly Beetle was bored with brooding, being tight-lipped, cold-eyed, and all alone. Whistling casually, he sauntered down the dune towards them.

"Hello," said Mrs Spooner, with no surprise, as if Beetle hadn't been ignoring them for days.

"What's been going on then?" asked Beetle

innocently, as if he hadn't been spying on their every move.

"Nothing much," admitted Abby. "The Council is still considering Mr Fishwick's offer."

"They're announcing their decision on Monday," added Mrs Spooner. "It'll probably be yes."

Beetle almost plunged again into a pit of deepest gloom. His lower lip began to slide out like a fat, pink slug...

"Don't you dare!" warned Abby. "Don't you dare start sulking again."

"I'm not sulking. I'm cheerful!" He looked earnestly around, searching for something cheerful to talk about.

"Look," he said in his best chirpy voice, "there's flowers growing there, where the Biosphere was!"

"Where?" Abby wrinkled her nose in a puzzled frown.

"There, look!"

On the charred earth, a scattering of

delicate flowers bloomed, like tiny pale stars.

"Good Lord," said Mrs Spooner. "He's right, Abby. And I never even noticed them. I've been so busy lately with this Save Our Ramshackles campaign."

Mrs Spooner peered at them with her sharp, inquisitive eyes. She dragged a hand lens from one of the many pockets of her dungarees. "You know, this might be a real discovery!"

Beetle sighed. "Only stupid flowers," he muttered crossly. "Nothing to get excited about!"

Curious, Abby got down on her knees to look closely at them. They weren't white, as she had first supposed, but the palest purple with a dark purple stripe on each petal. At the base of each flower the six petals joined to form a deep cup and in the cup were three bright yellow spikes.

Beetle threw a brief, careless glance at the tiny stars as if to say: "How boring!" But, despite himself, something tugged in his mind. He scowled, trying to remember. It was something about those papery-thin purple petals.

Beetle felt left out again as Abby and Mrs Spooner talked excitedly. He almost slouched off to the safety of the dunes. In fact he was on his way, backing into the shade of the sycamores, when Mrs Spooner rapped at him, "Come back here!"

"Wha–what, me?" stammered Beetle. He thought he'd done something terribly wrong

"Well done!" boomed Mrs Spooner. "Well done, Beetle!" she cried again, her pointy chin spiking the air as she nodded emphatically.

"Eh?" Beetle said to himself, bemused.

Reluctantly he sidled out from under the sycamores.

"It's a sand crocus!" beamed Mrs Spooner, tucking the lens away and buttoning up her pocket. "I'm almost certain of it. *Romulea columnae* is its proper name. And it's a wonderful find. It might just be the answer to all our problems!"

"Eh?" repeated Beetle blankly.

"Well, it's very, very rare. It only grows in one other place in the entire country! It's a protected flower. Nobody's allowed to pick it, or dig it up."

"That's right," interrupted Abby eagerly. "It's a brilliant find, Beetle. Brilliant!"

Beetle had no idea what they were talking about.

"You see," continued Mrs Spooner, "you can't disturb it in any way. So, if I'm right, no one can lay a finger on these sand dunes now we've found it. Not even Maurice Fishwick."

Beetle's face creased into an angry, bewildered frown. Events were rushing on too fast for him. He couldn't grasp why she was making all this fuss about a little purple flower. A flower you wouldn't even notice if it wasn't growing in a starry crowd inside a burnt-out Biosphere.

"I don't know what's going on!" he blurted out, indignantly. He hated it when he didn't know what was going on.

"Don't you see, Beetle?" prompted Abby.

"The dunes are no use to Maurice Fishwick any more. He can't bulldoze them – or build on them. And all because of this sand crocus you found."

"There's a lot to do, though," warned Mrs Spooner, scribbling lists in a notebook she'd hauled from one of her many pockets. "Have to get in touch with the right people. Get our discovery made official. Then get these dunes declared a nature reserve. They won't be safe until we do that."

She turned to Abby. "There must be other sand crocuses growing in these dunes. But I've never seen one. I bet most years only a handful of them ever flower. Rabbits nibble at the roots, or the frost gets them. Things like that. Your Biosphere protected these. Kept them safe and warm. That's why there's so many of them flowering. Beautiful, aren't they?"

Abby said nothing. She was just deeply relieved that something good had come out of the Biosphere after all.

Beetle almost protested: My grandpa found one! My grandpa found one of those crocus things! He had understood at last. He remembered now about the message and the purple flakes that he had shaken out of the newspaper article. He realized that he'd thrown away the most important part of the message – a sand crocus, which his grandpa must have found out on the dunes and had carefully pressed and kept inside his wallet.

But Beetle kept his mouth shut. He could see, now, why his grandpa had sent the message to Mrs Spooner. Those dried-out purple petals that he had brushed onto the floor would have made sense to her.

Beetle scowled at his own stupid jealousy.

"Don't look so miserable, Beetle!" commanded Abby. "You've done something wonderful. You've saved the Ramshackles!"

Beetle glared at her, suspiciously, as if she were making fun of him. His idea of saving the Ramshackles had been something altogether more heroic than finding a fragile purple flower. He had imagined himself crashing into action like Cryotron or Epidemon. "Watch out, it's Beetle!" his enemies would shriek, scattering in all directions...

"Congratulations, Beetle," said Mrs Spooner warmly. "Your grandpa will be proud."

And, suddenly, magically, Beetle found that he quite liked her. He even liked her floppy dungarees. He couldn't understand why he'd ever seen her as a barmy old witch, picking through her bones.

Instead, as hot water gurgles round the radiator when you switch on the central heating, Beetle felt his chest, his neck, his face, even the scalp on his head heating up. He was blushing. "I've saved the Ramshackles!" he told himself in an awed voice. "I, Beetle, kept my promise!" For the first time in days his mouth stretched into a joyous grin.

"Yay!" He punched the air. "I, Beetle, am invincible!"

Chapter 9

It was weeks before Beetle and Abby met again.

Spring flowers like the sand crocus had given way to summer flowers. Sea lavender and evening primrose blossomed all over the dunes.

Beetle grew three inches taller. Stick Insect and Red-hair were picked up by the police, wrecking a children's playground. Abby had the brace taken off her teeth.

Grandpa came home from hospital and rested, with his bad leg stretched out in front of him like a giant white maggot. Beetle got Predator back. But he never found his other lost warriors.

Nothing happened to Maurice Fishwick. He was still in his glass cage, surrounded by machines that glowed and babbled in the dark.

But at least he hadn't got his hands on the Ramshackles.

The Ramshackles, for the time being, were safe. The dunes weren't going to be sold to him, or to anyone else. And there was much talk of making them into a nature reserve. Mrs Spooner had done her work well – there had been lots of publicity. For weeks, while the rare sand crocus bloomed, her back yard had been trampled by people who came to admire it. The local newspapers had written a feature about it. Even the television people were interested in it. For a time, the Ramshackles had been quite famous. Now the sand crocus had gone until next spring. Fresh grass had grown on the scorched earth. And you couldn't tell that Abby's Biosphere had ever existed.

On the first day of the summer holidays, Beetle came dashing past Mrs Spooner's bone collection. She was kneeling on her front porch gazing into a bucket of seawater. It had a jellyfish in it – a tiny transparent umbrella pulsing in and out like a heartbeat.

"Hello!" gasped Beetle as he raced by.

"Wait a minute!" said Mrs Spooner.

Beetle skidded to a halt.

"I've hardly seen you these last few weeks. What have you been doing, Beetle? Working hard at school? Busy with your homework?"

"Not exactly," said Beetle.

When he looked back, he couldn't really say what he'd been doing. Helping his grandpa, running errands for him until he got the plaster cast taken off his leg. But what else? Of course, he'd been doing some Adventure Gaming. But somehow he wasn't so keen on that any more. He couldn't seem to get involved. It was yesterday's craze. He was ready for a new craze now.

But he still carried Predator in his pocket. Just for luck.

"Is Abby here yet?" asked Beetle, hopping impatiently from one foot to the other.

"Yes. She's on the beach, doing some kind of experiment." Mrs Spooner chuckled. "She's been carrying things down there all morning. You know, I even thought I saw her dragging an old bed down there. I must have been seeing things!"

"Right!" said Beetle. "Right! I'll be off then. See what she's up to." And he shot away again.

Beetle threaded along mossy tracks down to the seashore. Bindweed flowers, big floppy white trumpets, tumbled over every bush. On the dune tops, the prickly scrub was dark and tangled – a shelter for skylarks, a wildwood for rabbits. Down in the slacks the cool pools of sand were deep, shadowy, mysterious. For the first time, Beetle really appreciated how terrible it would have been if all this had been bulldozed flat...

Suddenly he popped out of the scrub onto a wide, flat, windy beach.

People didn't use this beach much. It was always spongy wet, with chilly gusts of wind chasing over it. Only Mrs Spooner was a regular visitor here – beachcombing for interesting bones.

"Abby!" yelled Beetle.

He couldn't see her anywhere. Along miles of sand, smooth and glazed as toffee, there seemed to be no one but himself. It was important to find Abby. Looking back, to when his grandpa was in hospital, he could see that he had been a pain – moping hopelessly around. He wanted to make amends, to be cheery, to persuade her that he wasn't moody like that *all* the time.

"Abby!" he cried.

"Here I am!" Her voice rushed towards him, almost drowned by a strange wubbering noise he couldn't identify. He turned round.

"Look out!"

Beetle gave a great springy leap like a frog and landed *crunch!* on his side on the sand. Winded, he struggled up on all fours and gaped, his mouth hanging open, along the beach. He forgot all about being cheery.

"Wait for me!" He struggled to his feet and began to lurch down the beach, trying to catch up with Abby.

"What is it?" he gasped, as the distance closed between them.

"What?"

"It's brilliant!"

"It's a sand yacht," said Abby. "It's my latest experiment."

She was sitting in the strangest vehicle Beetle had ever seen.

"You nearly ran over me just now!"

"Oh, sorry," said Abby, "but I couldn't see you. There are still some minor technical hitches."

Beetle prowled cautiously round the sand yacht. It seemed to be constructed of a bed made of some silvery metal, perched high on four wheels.

"Is that a— ?" began Beetle.

"Yes," interrupted Abby eagerly. "It's an old camping bed. Very light. Aluminium. Someone had thrown it away. So I rescued it. And, look, two of these are bike wheels and the other two are from a baby's pram."

In front of the yacht, collapsed upon the sand like a giant jellyfish, was a mass of plastic. It was attached to the aluminium frame by four long nylon chords. Beetle nudged it with his foot. "What's this?"

"That's the spinnaker. Like ships have. It's a sort of sail to catch the wind. Remember those plastic sheets that I used for the Biosphere walls? Well, this is one that I had left over."

Beetle frowned. As he'd hurled himself aside just now he'd glimpsed something flapping and silver-grey whipping past his face. He'd wondered why it seemed familiar.

"There's just one or two little snags," explained Abby. "For instance, when the wind fills up the spinnaker, you can't see where you're going. That's why I nearly ran you over just now."

"Humm." Beetle pursed his lips, thinking hard about this problem. He imagined Abby in her sand yacht, rocketing blindly along the beach, mowing down anyone in her way...

"Well," he finally admitted, "that *is* a tiny disadvantage. But so what? All you need to do is stay on this beach, where there aren't many people. And your problem's solved!"

That was the thing he liked about being with Abby. She was a positive thinker. And when she got thrilled about a project, you couldn't help being thrilled about it too. You believed that almost anything was possible.

"What I really need," said Abby, "is to buy some clear plastic, so I can see through it like a window. But I've got no money."

Beetle shrugged regretfully. He was always broke. He knew, without bothering to look, that the only thing in his pocket was Predator.

Excitedly, he knelt to inspect the sand yacht more closely. It was straining to take off. The wires in the bed-frame thrummed like a guitar. The sail was squirming on the ground, lifting, falling again as the wind crept underneath it.

"Want a go?" asked Abby.

"You bet!" Beetle grinned – he thought she'd never ask him. He could feel a new craze coming on!

A tiny doubt did itch inside his mind. The Biosphere, the Solar Furnace: they had been spectacular, ambitious. But both of them had got out of control. As if they had minds of their own. The Biosphere had sprung all sorts of nasty, as well as nice, surprises. And the Solar Furnace had refused to work when they wanted it to – but had sneakily performed once their backs were turned.

Still, thought Beetle, third time lucky. And the sand yacht was beautifully simple – just a light metal frame, four wheels and a sail. What could possibly go wrong? As Abby got off the sand yacht, Beetle climbed aboard.

"You sit here. On this bit of wood," explained Abby. "And put your feet on here. But you'll have to scoot it first, until the wind gets in the spinnaker."

"Right, right!" Beetle barely listened. He was longing to get going. Longing to tear along the sand, break the sound barrier, accelerate to warp speed and blast through into hyperspace. The bed-frame twitched and shuddered, as anxious as he was to leap into action.

"Brilliant!" Beetle kept muttering.

"Brilliant!" He thought Abby was a genius.

Abby, her arms outstretched, grappled with the sail, holding it aloft like a giant kite, to catch the wind.

"Right. Off you go!"

"Brilliant!"

Eagerly Beetle crouched like a jockey on the bed-frame, scooting it along. It was so light. It flew. It skimmed over sand like a pond-skater on water. Abby stumbled in front, her arms overflowing with sail.

The sail began to quiver restlessly. Then it bulged into a great swollen belly. Suddenly it tore free from Abby's grasp, soaring skywards, straining at the end of its ropes like a living thing.

"We have lift-off!" screamed Beetle.

The sand yacht sprang forward with Beetle clinging grimly to its rattling metal frame. The wind was booming in his ears. It was dragging his hair back by the roots, stretching his face like Playdoh into a grinning mask.

"One last snag," said Abby.

But Beetle was gone. Whisked away. Shooting like a bullet down the beach. The wheels were a blur. The sand yacht glittered – the spinnaker swooping above it like a greating silver bird with a diamond in its claws.

"Beautiful," breathed Abby.

"Yayyy!" She could hear Beetle's wild, exultant cry, faintly from a long way away.

"One last snag," said Abby to empty air, "is that I haven't worked out a braking system yet."

She had only come to a halt because the wheels of the sand yacht had got tangled up in driftwood.

"Perhaps," she mused, "he'll have the sense to use the spinnaker to steer with. Perhaps he'll have the sense to drag his foot along the ground to slow it down."

But Beetle didn't have the sense to do any of these things. He hadn't thought about stopping. At the moment he was busy shrieking with excitement and clinging on for dear life.

Abby shaded her eyes. Beetle was already a speck in the distance. Now he was lost in the trembling heat haze – streaking towards the popular beaches, crammed with unsuspecting holiday-makers. Abby shrugged helplessly.

"He'd better not crash!" she was thinking. "He'd better not crash and wreck my sand yacht!"